FORGET ME NOT

Griffin Force 3.5

JULIE COULTER BELLON

Other Books by Julie Coulter Bellon

Canadian Spies Series

Through Love's Trials

On the Edge

Time Will Tell

Doctors and Dangers Series

All's Fair

Dangerous Connections

Ribbon of Darkness

Hostage Negotiation Series

All Fall Down (Hostage Negotiation #1)

Falling Slowly (Hostage Negotiation #1.5)

Ashes Ashes (Hostage Negotiation #2)

From the Ashes (Hostage Negotiation #2.5)

Pocket Full of Posies (Hostage Negotiation #3)

Forget Me Not (Hostage Negotiation #3.5)

Ring Around the Rosie (Hostage Negotiation #4)

Griffin Force Series

The Captive

The Captain

The Capture

ACKNOWLEDGMENTS

Thank you to Dawn, Jon, Robyn, and Annette who are the best beta readers, critique partners, and all around most amazing people an author could know.

Thank you to my SWAT team who make me laugh and keep me going through thick and thin.

And thank you to my family. You are everything.

CHAPTER ONE

For the past few hours, Detective Bart Gutierrez had been living on adrenaline and he knew the crash was coming. The hostage situation had ended peacefully, but it had been touch and go most of the day. After stopping to park in front of his mother's flower shop, he rested his forehead against the steering wheel. Sucking in a breath, he let it out slowly. He never wanted to bring his work home with him, to have the things he saw and experienced touch the people he loved. Today was no different.

Maybe I should just go home. But his mom was providing all the flowers for a big wedding reception this afternoon, and he wanted to help her get the heavier ones inside. *At least that's part of it.* As weary as he was, he wanted to see Lucy. The thought of her smile made all the edginess of the last few hours fade away. They'd only been home from Colombia for a month, but she already dominated his thoughts. Before, he didn't mind staying late or covering a shift. Now he couldn't wait to be with her. And if that meant he spent more time delivering flower arrangements, then that's what he'd do.

He got out of the car and headed in to Forget Me Not, the bell over the door tinkling when he opened it. Satisfaction rolled through him knowing his mom now owned the shop outright. She'd worked here for years and was finally living her dream of being a business owner. "Ma? You here?"

She came out of the back carrying a large vase filled with tall cylindrical-looking flowers and peeked from behind it. "Right here. Thanks for coming to help me, *mijo*."

He laughed and took the vase from her. "I can hardly see you behind that thing. What kind of flowers are they?"

"Calla lilies on top with hydrangeas on the bottom layer. Aren't they beautiful?" She buried her nose in the arrangement. "The bride chose them for all the centerpieces."

"They're so big. How will people be able to see each other across the tables?" Bart asked as he set it on the counter.

When it was safely anchored, he turned back to face his mother. She was small, her hair pulled back into a serviceable bun, her uniform of black pants and a white shirt that said Forget Me Not on the pocket still looking as fresh as when she'd put it on. There wasn't anything out of place, the entire ensemble made to help her blend into the background. But, as usual, she wore her special flower earrings that made her stand out from anyone else. Today it was large purple pansies. She always wore those particular ones when she felt happy and confident, and it made him feel good to see that.

"We do what the bride wants. And besides, once you're sitting, the only thing in the way is the vase." She turned to grab a box on the floor. "We better start loading up."

He looked around the shop. "So, where's Lucy?" Bart asked, trying to keep his voice nonchalant. His mother was well-meaning, but she'd been in matchmaker overdrive since he brought Lucy home. Knowing her, she'd probably already decided on all the flower arrangements for their wedding—and centerpieces for their future children's christenings. Of course with how strong his feelings were for Lucy, those things were definitely in his mind for the future, but they'd just started exploring their relationship and still had some figuring out to do.

"Someone looking for me?" Lucy came out of the back room, holding an arrangement identical to the one his mother had, but since she was a little taller, she wasn't quite so hidden behind the towering flowers and her head was visible. She wore the same bun as his mother, but some tendrils had come loose and were curling just at the nape of her neck, a soft spot he liked to touch himself.

She crossed the room to him and set down the flowers, bringing his attention back to her face. For a second it looked like she might reach for him, but changed her mind at the last second. Bart squelched his disappointment.

"I'm surprised to see you here. That hostage scene was all over the news. It looked pretty bad. I thought for sure you'd go straight home," she said, searching his eyes.

Bart put his hands in his pockets so he wouldn't be tempted to reach out and touch her hair. Or her face. Or just hug her. "I'll sleep after we unload all of these." He nodded toward the boxes and vases covering the floor and counter space.

"Well, I won't say no to your help," his mother said as she reached up on tiptoe and kissed him on the cheek. "Thank you."

She bustled out to the van with a box of glass vases. Bart bent to pick up a calla lily arrangement, but Lucy stopped him with a hand on his arm. "Are you okay? From what I saw, no one expected that situation to have a happy ending."

"Yeah, it was a tough one." Bart looked down into her brown eyes, seeing worry and concern there. For him. His chest tightened. As kids, she'd annoyed him, getting under his skin with her constant challenges in sports, bike races, and even watermelon seed-spitting. Even with all that, though, she'd still managed to end up being one of his best friends. Together with her and Manny, they'd been the Three Musketeers, willing to take on anything or anyone.

It still amazed him that he'd found Lucy again after losing touch for all those years. His feelings from childhood had turned into so much more. She got under his skin in a whole new way and, so far, the adult Lucy was full of surprises. Sometimes she reminded him of that daredevil young girl she'd been, and other times she kept her cards close to the vest. She was a beautiful, complex woman who'd been through so much and come out stronger. The kind of woman he'd been searching for and was lucky enough to have in his life again.

"Bart?" She waved her hand in front of his face. "Where'd you go?"

Realizing he'd been staring, he stepped back and tried to pick up the conversation. "Sorry. You distract me."

She lightly slapped his shoulder. "Be serious."

He held up his hands and chuckled. "I am." She raised her eyebrows, and he sobered. "All right, I was just going to say the whole thing would have been over a lot sooner if the guy hadn't been coming off a high. It's tough to reason with people on drugs." And it had taken nearly thirty hours before they'd gotten the girlfriend out safely. With how agitated the guy had been it was a miracle no one had been killed.

Lucy let out a little puff of air, her concern turning to sympathy. "I'm glad it ended well. I've seen way too many situations where it didn't."

Her words brought Bart back to the reality he'd compartmentalized in an out-of-the-way place in his head. Their connection to a drug cartel wouldn't be going away anytime soon. He couldn't change who his father was, and Lucy had been an undercover operative for years.

No doubt she'd seen her share of tragedy while in the Castillo cartel. Hopefully being here with him would help put that behind her, though, so they could both move on. "I hope the guy gets some help," he said finally. But he didn't want to talk shop anymore. With her so close, he couldn't control the temptation he'd had since she'd come in, and he reached out to cup her face. "I've been looking forward to seeing you all day."

She pressed her cheek into his palm. "I'm glad you're here. Safe."

"Do you worry about me then?" Her skin was so silky soft; he let his thumb trail over her cheek and down her neck.

"Maybe a little. It would be just our luck to survive Colombia, only to have you get shot on the job in Connecticut." Her breaths were coming faster, and he could feel her pulse thrumming under his fingers.

He moved closer, unable to take his eyes off of her. "Maybe our luck is changing," he said, just as he bent to kiss her.

Before he could, he heard his mother's familiar steps behind them. Lucy jumped back, and they both turned. His mother was standing there with an indulgent smile. "Don't mind me."

Bart rolled his eyes, but his lips curved in amusement at his mother's dramatics. "I won't, Ma." He leaned closer to Lucy and kissed her forehead. "Later."

Lucy smiled and grabbed a smaller arrangement. "I'm counting on it."

They went out to the van, and it didn't take long before everything was loaded. "Should I follow you over to the reception hall?" Bart asked his mother.

"That's a good idea. You know what's a better idea? If Lucy goes with you in your car. Then I can play my music loud." She winked and climbed into the driver's seat of the floral van, starting it up and not waiting for an answer.

Lucy laughed. "Hey, I don't mind your music." But Daniela was already pulling away. They watched her leave and Lucy brushed her hands together. "Well, that was pretty obvious."

Bart grinned. "That's why I love her." He took advantage of the opportunity to pick up where they'd left off by pulling her against him. She smelled like a smorgasbord of all of his favorite flowers, and he drew in a deep breath. "How are things going? Is it okay living with my mom for now?" Not exactly an ideal situation, but until they could find her an apartment nearby, it was the most logical.

"Things are fine," she said, drawing back slightly to look at him. Her words were the ones he wanted to hear, but there was a shadow in her eyes when she spoke.

Bart furrowed his brows, wanting to chase the shadows away. "That doesn't sound fine."

"How can I explain?" She dropped her chin and nestled her face into his chest. He liked the contact, but he also knew the signs. She didn't want to look him in the eye.

Avoidance wasn't like Lucy at all. She was the strongest woman he knew and always met every challenge head on. He loosened his hold to lift her face. "You can trust me. If it's not working out, we can find somewhere else for you to live." She closed her eyes, and a tear escaped. Bart's stomach dropped to the pavement as he wiped away the drop of moisture from her cheek. Was she having second thoughts? Was this new life too much? "Tell me, Luce."

She opened her eyes still shimmering with tears, and bit her lip. "It's just been so long since I had a mother." Her hands slid up his chest and around his neck, and he embraced her, relieved. "Your mom treats me like a daughter. I didn't realize how much I missed that."

Her voice was muffled against his shirt, and he could feel her trembling. "You can borrow my mom anytime. I don't mind sharing."

She gave him a sniffle-laugh, but stayed in his embrace. He tucked her head under his chin and stroked her hair, gratitude replacing the anxiety of a moment ago. She'd confided in him and was letting him give her comfort. With the way she'd bottled up her emotions for so long, he knew that was a gift.

Bart kissed the top of her head. "I know you had it rough growing up, but you've got a family now. Remember that." And he'd do all he could to make that permanent. Sooner rather than later, if he got his wish.

She held on for a moment longer, then pulled back. "Well, we better get going before we test that theory. Your mom will be wondering where we are."

"No, she won't." Bart gave her a quick kiss on the lips and opened the passenger door for her. "She's probably hoping we take a quick trip to Vegas." Lucy's eyes widened, and Bart felt his ears start to burn, a flush creeping up his neck. "You know how she is," he said lamely. He didn't want to bring up marriage before she was ready and have Lucy feel pressured. As it was, his mother's machinations were enough.

She touched his chin, a smile on her face. "I love everything about your mom."

What about me? he wanted to ask, but didn't. "I do, too. Most of the time," he deadpanned.

Lucy chuckled as she sat down in his car and wiped away her tears. "She's a romantic at heart. That's what makes her an exceptional florist."

And she wants you for a daughter-in-law, Bart added silently, suddenly wishing they didn't have anything to work out. Not many other couples had father issues like theirs—his father, head of a drug cartel, had ordered the murder of Lucy's father, who'd helped hide Bart and his mother. Could they get past that sort of baggage? Best to take things slow, but that was proving harder than he'd thought.

He got into the driver's seat and pulled into traffic, giving her a sidelong glance. Her hands were folded in her lap, and she was looking out the window. He hadn't known her to be so thoughtful before and wished he could read her thoughts. For some reason, whether lack of sleep was getting to him, or he was just over-thinking things, her demeanor had his anxiety antennae on full alert. "Besides being mothered 24/7, how is it working at the flower shop? My mom tells me you've won over Mr. Beagley, so you must be working some sort of magic there, but I'm sure customer service is pretty tame compared to what you're used to."

"Mr. Beagley was gruff, but it was all a show." She turned and smiled. "He was pretty tight-lipped at first, but I finally got him to open up to me."

"Mom said no one has ever been able to get a word out of him beyond hello and good day. You're a miracle-worker."

"When I was undercover I learned all kinds of ways to get people to talk." She lowered her voice as if imparting a great secret. "But I didn't have to use those techniques. Mr. Beagley is just a lonely old man who comes in every day to buy a flower for his wife's grave. When he saw I truly cared, well, that was all he needed."

"Working at a flower shop is a far cry from being undercover." Bart was pushing, but part of him had to know. Coming back to a normal life after being "under" had been too much for some cops he knew. He didn't want that for Lucy.

"I'm fine, Bart. You don't have to worry." She reached for his hand. "After watching over my shoulder every second for so long, making flower arrangements is a nice change. A happy change."

"Glad to hear it." He hadn't known until that moment how glad he really was. Bart gave her a smile and entwined his fingers with hers. Her hand was a little cold, so he rubbed his thumb over the back of it.

Lucy turned her knees toward him and squeezed his hand. "Okay, now who's getting people to talk? Your turn. You've been acting weird since you came in, and I know that case affected you. Can you tell me about it?"

Thinking back on how tense the hostage situation was and how he didn't want that feeling bleeding over into this part of his life, he grimaced. The weight of trying to balance his worlds crashed over him, especially since this was his first hostage situation since Colombia. The fact that drugs were the center of the case had brought up so many feelings he hadn't been prepared for. "I just wish I could put the past behind me. Let go of things." He clenched his jaw. How could he describe exactly how he felt without too many details? "Being up close and personal with how drugs affect people and families makes me think—" He stopped. His thoughts were probably silly or wouldn't make sense.

"You feel responsible somehow because of who your father was?" she asked gently. "Bart, you're nothing like him. Look at what you've done with your life. Almost the exact opposite. And you have no control over your father's actions."

Bart's hand clenched the wheel. "I don't want people to know my father was Nico Castillo. Especially anyone in law enforcement. I feel their judgment, see them wonder if I'm dirty and helping my father's cartel move the drugs, you know? He ruined so many people's lives, including yours." He stared straight ahead, his pulse starting to pound in his ears. "Most of the time I'm okay with it, but when hostage situations like this come up, it's hard to compartmentalize."

She didn't say anything, just moved closer until they were as close to shoulder-to-shoulder as they could be while seat-belted in a car—like a show of silent solidarity between the two of them. No one understood better than her that it would take time to process everything that had happened with Nico. Just having her support meant the world.

He lifted her hand to his lips and kissed the back of it. "Thanks for being here."

"Always. You just need time. We all do." She laid her head on his shoulder, and suddenly the burdens he'd been carrying seemed lighter with her at his side.

Too soon, they pulled into the parking lot of the reception hall. The Forget Me Not van was near a side entrance, and Bart pulled up next to it, wishing he hadn't used their precious time together to talk about his father. At the same time, though, if they were going to move forward, they had to be open and honest with each other.

"You know, I'm mostly feeling good about things when it comes to my dad and how his actions have affected me. Sometimes it's hard to have my integrity questioned." He ran a hand through his hair. "I'm just tired."

Lucy shook her head. "I worked for your father for five years, and I question myself sometimes. Maybe I should have done things differently. Stopped him sooner. Maybe even been more compassionate at the end." She leaned over the console and gave him a quick kiss on the cheek.

"Second-guessing yourself never does any good. Neither does questioning the man you are because of what your dad did. Or caring what others think they know about you. But I'm always here to listen if you need to talk about it. You've got a family, too. Don't forget that."

She tossed his own words back at him and his heart skipped a beat.

"I'm counting on it." He put the car into park and turned the last inch to press her to him, his mouth finding hers. Her hand came up to stroke his jaw, and combined with her soft lips exploring his, everything else faded away and there was only her—them.

"I'm falling in love with you, you know," he whispered when they came up for air.

"I'm already there," she whispered back.

He wanted to kiss her again, to show what those words really meant to him, but out of the corner of his eye he could see his mother waving to them. With a deep sigh, he knew his time alone with Lucy was over for the moment, but he was glad for what they'd had. "Are we going to pick this up later?" he asked in a low voice.

Lucy reached for the door handle, but smiled over her shoulder. "Definitely."

He got out and followed behind her as they joined his mother. These two women meant more to him than anything else in the world, and seeing Lucy in their little circle brought a grin to his face.

Family. He liked the sound of that.

CHAPTER TWO

Lucy watched the bride and groom dance one more time before they headed off to their honeymoon. They only had eyes for each other. Obviously they were very much in love and she put her hand on her heart at the same moment a shiver of unease went up her spine. It was like she didn't want to allow herself to feel happiness. She looked away and sat down in a satin-covered chair. She'd honed her ability to mask her feelings and vulnerabilities while undercover, and adjusting to normal life was something she hadn't allowed herself to think about. But now she was living it.

She looked up at the twinkling white lights strung across the ceiling and thought about Bart. He'd been her light through some dark times. They'd both been through so much and he was right—the heartache all led back to his father, Nico. Brushing aside her own issues with the man, seeing Bart struggle to come to terms with who his father was had been difficult to watch. He wasn't anything like Nico. Bart's heart was in the right place, but nothing she said could make him believe that. He had to find his own answers. At least he was talking his feelings through with her and he sought her out every spare moment he had. Her heart warmed at the thought. Together they could do anything.

Daniela came and sat beside her, crossing her ankles. "You did a great job with the flower arrangements tonight. Everything is perfect."

"Thanks." She scooted closer to the older woman and slipped an arm around her shoulders. "Have I told you how much I appreciate everything you've done for me since I came home?"

Daniela clucked her tongue. "I'm glad to hear you call this your home. I want you to think that way." She patted Lucy's cheek. "You were always such a sweet girl. Good for my boy, especially when he hurts." She touched her chest. "Here."

Lucy's eyes dropped. She'd suspected Daniela knew he was having difficulties regarding his father, even though Bart was trying to keep it to himself. "I love him," she said simply. Daniela's smile grew nearly as wide as her face, the words obviously what she'd wanted to hear, but Lucy held up a hand. "But we have things to work through before we can go anywhere."

Daniela waved a hand in the air as if sweeping away any problems. "You can work through things after you are married and settled."

Lucy laughed. "One step at a time."

"All right," Daniela grumbled good-naturedly. She looked at her watch. "Are you ready to go home?"

"I might need someone to carry me to the van," Lucy groaned. "I should have worn my running shoes."

"I can call Bart back if you like," Daniela said with a twinkle in her eye. "I'm sure he won't mind."

She moved her hand to her pocket where she always kept her phone, but Lucy grabbed her arm. "No, let him sleep. He needs it."

Daniela's expression turned serious. "You're right, after that last shift, my son needs sleep. But he needs love more. And to know he doesn't have to hide things from me. I want to help. We've been so close all of his life. Does he think I can't tell he's working through something? It's his father, isn't it?" She looked Lucy in the eye, searching her face, looking for the answer there.

Lucy put her hand over Daniela's. "He just needs some time, that's all."

Daniela blew out a breath. "I wish I could make it better. I wish I could go back and change the past."

"Bart will get through this," Lucy soothed. "He's a strong man, and you are a big reason for that. Trust him now."

"You're a good girl." Daniela drew her hand away and patted Lucy's shoulder. "I will try to be patient. With both of you." She moved away to the table behind them, brushing some crumbs off of it, before heading to the exit. Lucy slowly stood and followed behind. She believed the words she'd told Daniela, but if she was being honest, they'd mostly been for her. *I just need more time to adjust, that's all.* But the longer she thought about things, the more frightened she got. It shouldn't be this easy to start over. To feel so happy. Those feelings were the root of the problem.

She'd bounced from one extreme to the other. In a matter of weeks, she'd gone from trying to get enough evidence to arrest the head of one of the largest drug cartels in the world, alone and looking over her shoulder every minute, to being in love, having a normal job and an almost-mother. It was scary to finally have light and contentment in her life. She wasn't sure how to react or if she could really go all in. There was so much on the line now. More than money or drugs or a job. Bart's words echoed in her head. She had a family.

She went around to the passenger side and got in, shivering a bit with cold. Or was it a tingle of fear? When she'd lost her parents as a teen, she lost herself for a while, too. Going undercover had seemed logical and trying to get revenge for her father's murder had given her a reason to get up in the morning. But now, losing her old life felt like shedding a skin that had been confining and oppressive. Having a family, people in her life that loved her, was freeing and made her heart soar, but it was also risky. What if she lost them, too? She'd picked herself up once after that happened, but it had nearly killed her. There was no way she could do it again and survive it. So what could she do?

As soon as they got going, the dark turn of her thoughts was swallowed up in an impromptu concert when Daniela turned up her favorite Julio Iglesias tune and started belting it out along with him.

Don't go looking for trouble, she told herself. *Enjoy this moment.* She wanted to join in, but her singing voice was the kind dogs howled along with, so she listened and tapped her feet with the music.

They turned the corner and headed toward Daniela's small, but comfortable, house. Lucy noticed a black sedan parked across the street, the kind that, in her experience, held unpredictable men in suits. That prickle of unease was back and her training to be aware of the details in any situation jumped into high gear. They pulled into the driveway, and Daniela held the last note of the song before she killed the engine. Two men got out of the sedan and started toward them. Lucy tensed, her eyes riveted on the mirror as she watched their movements. Just as she suspected, they were dressed in suits, but that didn't mean they were good guys.

She touched Daniela's arm trying to keep her voice calm and even. "Call Bart. And stay in the car." She wished she had her gun. Just in case.

Daniela followed her gaze and saw the men. Her hand clutched Lucy's arm. "Don't go out there. Stay in here and wait for Bart with me." Daniela's hand trembled as she drew back and took out her phone. "I'm calling the police, too."

"It will be all right. I'll just see what they want." Lucy's stomach did a flop. Had thinking about losing a family brought bad karma from the universe?

Don't be ridiculous, she told herself.

Lucy got out of the car and smoothed down her Forget Me Not work shirt. Walking around the van, she met them in the middle of the lawn. "Good evening, gentleman. Can I help you?"

The man closest to her looked like a body builder, with his arm muscles straining his suit jacket and his neck barely visible. "We're from Homeland Security. We'd like to speak with Daniela Gutierrez. Is that her in the car?"

Lucy sidestepped the question, but made sure she got between them and the van. "Can I see some identification?"

Both men stopped walking and held out their IDs to her. The bodybuilder was Special Agent Furniss, and the poster boy for the military was his partner, Special Agent Allen. He'd likely been in the service with his short blond hair, clean-shaven jaw and shoes polished to perfection. Neither of their ID pictures were more than a glorified mug shots, really, but from all appearances they were from Homeland Security. What did they want with Daniela? With her background, it made more sense they'd be here for Lucy.

After taking another minute to look the IDs over, she'd hopefully given Bart enough time to be on his way over. "What's this about, Agent Furniss?"

"I'm afraid we can only talk to Ms. Gutierrez about that." Furniss started toward the van again, and Lucy signaled to Daniela that it was okay to get out. She carefully opened the door, her eyes darting between the two men. Maybe they could ask their questions and be on their way, but Lucy stayed close on Furniss's heels. He wasn't going to intimidate Daniela if she could help it.

"Ms. Gutierrez, you've been flagged for terroristic activities. I'm afraid we're going to have to ask you to come down to the field office." Furniss stopped in front of Daniela and gave her a stern expression.

"Terroristic activities?" She squeaked out. Her hand fluttered to her neck. "I don't know what you're talking about. I'm an honest business owner."

He reached out to take her arm, but Daniela stepped out of his reach and he scowled. "I think you know what we're talking about. It's people like you immigrating here, lying low until the time is right to strike, that give honest business owners a bad name," he ground out.

"Time to strike? What do you think, that I put bombs in flowers?" Daniela put her hands on her hips and faced the guy down. "That's ridiculous."

He raised his eyebrows. "Is that a confession?" He turned to his partner. "Did you hear that?"

Lucy quickly walked forward and stood between them. "Can't this wait until morning? I'll be happy to keep her in my custody, especially since it looks like we should contact a lawyer."

"She won't need a lawyer." Furniss was faster this time; he grabbed Daniela's arm. "I was going to say if you come quietly, this likely won't take long, but you've given a statement that could be construed as a threat and we'll be taking you with us tonight."

Daniela cried out in alarm and tried to pull away, but he yanked her close. "Quiet."

Lucy took Daniela's other arm. "Let her go. Now." They were caught in a tug of war, but Lucy didn't care. What if these men weren't who they purported to be? Even with their IDs, her intuition said Daniela shouldn't go anywhere with this guy.

Furniss gripped Daniela's arm hard enough to leave a bruise and then shook her, obviously trying to make Lucy lose her grip. All it did was push Lucy into action. She had to protect Daniela. Letting go, she took a step forward for momentum before she power-punched Furniss in the throat.

He bent over gasping and dropped Daniela's arm. Lucy turned as Allen ran toward her. She got down into her fighting stance, ready for a drop kick if he came anywhere near either of them. Before she could do anything, though, she heard the screech of tires and Bart's voice ringing out. "Police! Step back and stand down! Now!"

Either Allen didn't hear Bart or didn't care, because he kept on coming like he was going to tackle her. Lucy shifted at the last second, just out of his reach and he stumbled with the force of his miss.

Before he could turn around, Bart was beside her. His mother ran into his arms and he held her close, shushing her cries. "It's okay, Ma, I'm here now." He looked between the three of them. "Will someone tell me what's going on here?"

Allen stood there, folding his arms, trying to look like he hadn't nearly face-planted in the front yard. "We're here to arrest your mother."

CHAPTER THREE

Bart escorted his mother and Lucy through the doors of the police station. This boxy, bustling place was like a second home to him, but he wasn't supposed to see any part of it for at least another twenty-four hours. He didn't know where else to go, though. There was no way he could let these agents take his mother to their field office. Who knew what restrictions would be in place there? He might even be denied access. At least at the station, he had a home-field advantage.

Furniss was still glaring at Lucy and Bart had kept her close—her on one side, his mother on the other. He still wasn't sure exactly what had happened before he arrived, but from the look of the bruise forming on Furniss's neck, Lucy had gotten in a good shot. Bart knew she wouldn't have done something like that unless she felt threatened, so the guy probably deserved it. He didn't seem anxious to press charges, so maybe deep down he knew he'd been in the wrong.

Before Bart had cleared the bull pen, Colby, his partner, met them. "The captain will be here shortly. Said you should wait in his office."

"I'm surprised to see you here," Bart said. Colby had been at his side through the entire hostage situation and had to be as tired as he was.

"When I heard that an incident was reported at your mom's place, I came right in." He looked over at the woman still clutching Bart's arm. "I'm sorry to hear there was trouble tonight, Mrs. Gutierrez."

Daniela patted Colby's cheek. "Thank you." Her voice was still breathy, and she seemed a little shaky.

"Would you mind getting her a coffee?" Bart asked. "This might take awhile."

"Sure thing." Colby ducked his head to glance at the agents standing just in front of Bart. "Any idea what's going on?"

"Just that they said they're going to arrest my mom." Bart wanted to swallow the words back. Even saying them made his stomach sour. His mother's grip tightened on his elbow and he reached over to pat her hand. "But that's not going to happen."

"Not on our watch," Colby agreed. "Can I bring you a coffee, too, Lucy?"

"That would be great, thanks."

Her voice was flat, and Bart turned to focus on her. She wasn't giving any feelings away through facial expressions. She looked like an undercover professional, keeping things casual but taking in all the details. He groaned inwardly, wanting the light back in her eyes, the warmth in them. They were going after the fresh start they both deserved. Hopefully they could get this Homeland issue figured out quickly and get back to that.

"I'll get your coffee," Colby said and headed toward the vending machine.

Bart continued on to the captain's office. He opened the door and the two agents went in, followed by his mother, then Lucy.

Colby joined them with two coffee cups in hand. He offered one to Lucy and Daniela. Bart glanced over at Lucy close to his mother, her arm around her to offer comfort. At least they were all together. *Us against the world.* Lucy sat at an angle that partially shielded his mother from seeing the agents. His fists clenched seeing how shaken up his mother looked. Hopefully the coffee would help calm her a bit.

Colby walked back to Bart standing near the door. "Want some moral support?"

"Thanks, man, but this has all got to be a misunderstanding." He shoulder-bumped Colby. "I appreciate you being here." They were like brothers and it was times like this that Bart was glad he had another family to get him through.

The captain came up behind Colby and looked over Bart's head. "Okay, I put in a few phone calls to Homeland to try and get the orders verified. I'm just waiting for them to call back. Let's get in there and see what these guys have to say for themselves."

"Yes, sir," was Bart's automatic reply.

The captain was a no-nonsense guy who was good at what he did. The one thing Bart could count on though, was that Captain Reed had his back. Always. It was comforting in a law-enforcement/family sort of way.

They both walked further into the room, and Bart went to stand next to Lucy while the captain went behind his desk and sat down. He nodded to the two agents at his left. "Gentleman, would you care to explain what exactly is going on?"

Furniss looked at Allen and shook his head slightly. Apparently he wasn't up for speaking just yet, so Allen took over. "We have orders to bring Ms. Gutierrez in for questioning. We've got evidence that she's involved in terror activities."

"That's outrageous." Bart spoke quietly, trying to keep his temper in check. Why would they trump up charges against his mother? This was crazy.

"She practically confessed when we were at her house." Allen sat up straight in his chair. "She poses a danger to the United States." He looked around the room as if daring anyone to disagree with him.

Two chairs away, Daniela went rigid at his words. "I confessed to nothing. It was sarcasm, which was obviously above your head. And I'm not a danger to anyone. I'm a florist!"

Allen frowned. "It's not your job, it's your connections. To the Castillo cartel."

"Her ex-husband is dead. She doesn't have any other connections." Bart reached for his mother's hand. It was ice cold.

"You might want to ask your mother about that." Allen gave him a self-satisfied smile.

A retort was on the tip of his tongue until Bart looked at Daniela, his gut twisting at her guilty expression. Something was very wrong. "What's he talking about, Ma?"

"I want to talk to you alone." All the color in her face had drained, and for a second, with the way she wilted before his eyes, he wondered if she was going to faint.

Allen looked triumphant at her words. He stood and Bart clenched his fist. It was too tempting to wipe that smirk off his face.

"We'll be right back," he said to Lucy. "Will you be okay?" Maybe he should take her with them.

Lucy nodded. "I'll be fine."

"Well, I'm not fine," Allen said as he took a step toward Daniela. "We should be privy to any communication she has regarding the case."

Bart put his body between them, not wanting the guy anywhere near his mother. Lucy must have had the same idea since she bracketed Daniela's other side.

"Sit down, Agent Allen," the captain ordered. "We'll sort this out our way."

"Our Special Agent in Charge is going to hear about this," Allen grumbled as he sat back down.

"Like I said, I've already got a call in." The captain was serene, and Bart knew he would hold down the fort while he had a sit-down with his mother. With a last glance at Lucy, who gave him another encouraging nod, he shut the door and led his mother to the smallest interrogation room they had.

He opened the door for her, and she stepped through, looking at the rectangular room that boasted a utilitarian table and two metal chairs. She bypassed the chairs completely and immediately began pacing. "I can explain."

Bart folded his arms and leaned against the wall. So many questions churned through his mind, but he'd learned early in his career that sometimes you got more information if you let the person talk.

"There's a cartel war brewing." She didn't meet his eyes, just looked at the floor as she took four steps away from him and four steps back.

"What does that have to do with you? Nico was your last connection to the cartel, and that one was flimsy at best."

She flicked a glance at him before she took another round of four steps up and back. "It's Manny. One of Nico's old employees lured him back to the island. Said he could take Nico's place since they were family, and then he could finally make something of himself." She rubbed her hands up and down her arms as if she was cold. "Manny liked the sound of that, and Maria called me in a panic. She wanted me to ask you to talk to him, but I couldn't. You're still struggling with what happened when you were in Colombia. I didn't want to add to that, so I've been trying to talk to him myself."

She stopped in front of him, her eyes on his, willing him to understand. "I don't want you drawn into that life, and I want Manny to go home to his mother. That's all. I'm not a danger to anyone . . . but Manny might be." She stopped in front of him and reached out her arms. "I'm sorry."

Bart drew her into a hug, stunned at what she'd just said. He wanted to tell her it would be all right, but he knew they weren't out of the woods. "When I left him, Manny was going to get help. He was on his way home."

"He never made it." His mother wiped her eyes. "It's the drugs. He can't kick the addiction, and this old employee offers them to him for free if he'll be the puppet head they want."

That made sense. Manny was Nico's nephew and with his cocaine habit he was an easy mark. But drawing his mother in was unacceptable. "So, we'll tell Homeland what's going on. This has nothing to do with you. Your phone calls were just as a favor to your sister, that's all."

"I don't think they'll believe me. What if they're using me as leverage somehow?"

The thought had crossed Bart's mind. They'd used that ploy to rope him into going undercover for the Castillo cartel in the first place. Homeland seemed really good at using their power to get people to do what they wanted. "Is there anything else I should know?"

Her shoulders sagged. "I have a bank account number

Nico gave me before he died. He set up a trust fund for you." She looked up at him, her forehead creased with worry. "It's a lot of money. Millions. And Manny wants it."

Bart ran his hands through his hair. This was bad. She'd been talking to the possible new leader of the Castillo cartel. And she was in possession of an account that had millions in it. She couldn't look worse. "Ma. Why didn't you tell me?"

"I was going to, but I didn't know how with all you were going through." She grabbed his forearm as he groaned in frustration and pulled until he looked at her. "I just wanted to do what's right for you."

"Ma, we've had this conversation before! When you kept my father's identity a secret, it made everything worse. Now you're keeping secrets again, and giving me the same excuse. I'm a grown man. You don't have to protect me!" He pulled away and stalked to the opposite corner of the room. "We need to get you a lawyer."

"I haven't done anything wrong." She sat down in the chair and held her head in her hands. "I can't even regret marrying Nico because it gave me you." Her eyes met his. "I always want to protect you. I'm not sorry for that. I *am* sorry that you can't understand my motivations."

Bart took a breath and crossed back to her. He pulled her out of her chair and hugged her again. "I know, Ma. I'm trying. But you have to promise me that you won't keep any more secrets. We need to face these things together."

She pressed her nose into his chest and sniffled. "I promise. From now on, no more secrets."

They stood a moment more before he took her hand. "I don't want you to say anything to these agents. I'm going to get us a lawyer and get it taken care of that way. They haven't followed protocol, and that fact will be on our side."

The door behind them opened, and they both turned as the captain, Lucy, and the two agents squeezed in, filling the room to capacity. "What's going on?" Bart tried to protect his mother from being crushed between him and the two agents. Lucy was still trying to make her way over to them. "We were on our way back."

No one answered, but Lucy was finally within reaching distance. She put her hand on his arm, but before she could say anything, the people in the room parted for a smaller man with a Napoleon-like bearing. He slowly made his way over until he stood in front of Bart's mother.

"Daniela Gutierrez, I am Special Agent in Charge Kyle Miller, and you are being taken into custody."

Bart put his arm around his mother. "We're getting a lawyer. You haven't followed procedure, and we have grounds to sue for harassment at the very least. She'll be going home with me."

Miller gave him a once-over. "I'm afraid things have escalated, and she's considered a threat to national security. Please stand back."

"This is ridiculous, and you know it. I had a deal with

Homeland that if I went undercover for you guys, my mother could never be touched." He heard his mother's gasp, but he didn't have time to explain the reasons for the deal. At some point, he'd definitely be eating his own words about no secrets between them.

"That deal was nullified the second she started calling cartel members and accepting money." The smaller man put his hand in his pocket and glared at Bart. It was easy to see he didn't like being challenged.

"We have explanations for that, but need to speak to a lawyer," Bart said, not wanting to aggravate the situation further, but wanting a chance to tell their side, especially when they had witnesses around.

"So you admit that it's true?" Agent Miller tilted his head in surprise.

Bart ground his teeth. "I'm not admitting anything. This is a case of extenuating circumstances."

Agent Miller sighed dramatically in disappointment. "That term seems to come up a lot in my line of work. And, of course, we'll be happy to hear all about these circumstances during our interrogation."

"You're not taking her anywhere," Bart bit out, his patience at its limit.

Agent Miller straightened to his full height, which came to about Bart's chin. "I could ruin your career. You are interfering with a federal investigation."

Captain Reed came up on Bart's left side and folded his arms. "Threatening his career in front of me is not a good idea."

Bart opened his mouth to tell Miller where to go, but before he could, his mother stepped forward. "Where will you take me?"

"To our field office in Hartford." He moved aside and held his hand out so Daniela could precede him. She stood there, as if she was considering it.

"No, Ma. We need to get a lawyer, make sure you're protected." He wished they had another moment alone to discuss what would come next, what he wanted for her. "We'll consider it, if I can come with her," Bart said finally, hoping for at least a compromise. He blocked Miller's view of Daniela.

Miller stepped to the side, just far enough to be able to see his mother. "She'll be in holding for tonight, and you can visit her in the morning. Standard procedure for flight risks, but I guarantee she'll be fine until you see her next."

"None of this is standard procedure, and you're not going to have her in holding all night. She has rights. We need time to get a lawyer." Bart's voice rose with every sentence and echoed through the interrogation room. His heart was thundering through his ears. He couldn't let them take her. This was wrong. All wrong.

Miller stepped back and folded his arms. "I'm afraid you don't have a choice. Not if you don't want to be arrested yourself for interfering." He glanced over at the captain. "Or at least be written up and have that on your permanent record. Maybe both."

"It's okay," Daniela said as she stepped between the two

men and put her hand on Bart's chest. "We will cooperate. I will go."

"No, you won't." Bart was adamant.

"I am your mother and I will go." She lifted her chin. "I won't have you risk yourself for me."

He opened his mouth to say something else, but she held up her hand and shook her head. The conversation was over.

"A wise choice," Miller commented, as he gave Bart one last look before taking Daniela's arm and heading for the door.

His two agents followed close behind as they walked out, but Daniela squeezed back through the doorway and blew Bart a kiss. "I'll see you tomorrow, *mijo*."

"Remember what we talked about," he answered, giving her a pointed look. *Don't say anything to anyone.* She nodded as if she could read his thoughts, and then she was gone.

Lucy slipped her hand into his, staring at the doorway, looking as stunned as he felt. "We're going to get this sorted out."

"In my office. Now." The captain turned on his heel, not looking back, but expecting them to follow.

Bart rubbed his hands over his eyes. He'd only had about three hours of sleep, and this was all starting to feel like some horrible nightmare. But when he looked down at the fear and worry in Lucy's eyes, he knew he was awake. This was real.

And he had to find a way to take care of it. Fast.

CHAPTER FOUR

The captain's office had been turned into a war room, and Lucy was glad to be part of it. She needed to do something, to help get Daniela back. Everyone had been given a different assignment. Bart was investigating the account his mother had told him about, making sure no one had access to it besides her, especially since she was being held for terrorist activities. If he could prove it was merely a trust fund, well, that would be a point in their favor. Of course, it looked bad with the cartel nearly detonating a chemical warhead on American soil two months ago, but this was Daniela. If she was the only one with access, they could point to her honest business dealings and the fact that she had no criminal history. Anyone who knew her would say the thought of her being involved in terrorism was ludicrous.

Lucy had reached out to her old handler at Homeland, James Argyle, but he hadn't picked up, so she'd left a message. They needed a better picture of what they were really facing with the irregularities that had already happened. At the very least, they needed to know if Miller was really who was over Daniela's case. But no one had returned the captain's calls to Homeland, either, and for now, it looked like an information lockdown.

She watched Bart as he talked on the phone with someone. He looked exhausted, the dark circles under his eyes testifying that he hadn't gotten the sleep he needed. But she knew it wouldn't do any good to suggest that he rest. Not when it came to his mother. There wasn't anything he wouldn't do for her and that was one of the things she loved about him.

Lucy stood and walked behind his chair, putting her hands on his shoulders and massaging the tension out of them. He leaned forward so she could have better access.

"Please have her call me," he said as he ended the phone call.

"No luck?" She pushed on some pressure points, and he let out a little moan.

"That feels so good." His head nearly touched the desk as he lowered his shoulders. "I left messages for my *tia*, Maria, to call me the moment she gets in. If anyone will have any more information, it will be her."

"Where would she be at this hour?" She looked at the clock on the wall in front of her. It was nearly one a.m.

"Apparently, she's drowning her sorrows over Manny." Bart shook his head. "Her oldest daughter said she's taking it pretty hard."

"That's awful. Watching your mother self-destruct in front of your eyes can affect you in ways you can't imagine." She thought of her own mother, who couldn't handle the death of her father and had eventually killed herself. It had taken years for Lucy to let go of the guilt she had for not being able to help her mom.

Lucy bent and hugged him from behind. She wouldn't let her past color her future. Daniela was a strong woman, and she'd get through this. Both she and Bart would make sure of that. "It's going to be okay, you know."

He pulled her arms tightly around his shoulders and let out a sigh. "I'm sorry about your mom and bringing up painful memories. I wish there were more I could do for Maria and her family, but they need more help than I can give. Even getting Manny back might not be enough to heal the wounds." He stood and turned, pulling Lucy into his embrace. "Thanks for staying with me."

They held each other like that for a minute, and Bart was so still, she wondered if he'd actually fallen asleep standing up, but when her cell phone rang, he straightened. She fished it out of her pocket and looked at caller ID. "It's James."

She answered, trying to keep tension out of her voice. If there truly was an information lockdown at Homeland over this, she needed to tread carefully. "James, thanks for returning my call."

"I'm surprised to hear from you. I thought after you finished up with the Castillo case, you were out." James sounded smug, and that was never a good sign.

"Something came up." Lucy rounded the desk and sat in the chair in front of it. "Homeland is questioning Daniela Gutierrez, Nico's ex-wife, about her association with the cartel. You know anything about that?"

"You're calling me for gossip on your new boyfriend's mother?" She could almost see the self-satisfied smile on his face. James loved having the upper hand, knowing something other people didn't. It made him feel powerful, but was a weakness when he'd been running the cartel task force.

"It's more than that. These agents aren't following protocol. They're manhandling her, demanding her immediate cooperation without a lawyer, taking her to a holding cell. I'd say she might have a case against the U.S. government for violating her rights." Lucy kept her voice even. She didn't want to threaten the guy, but she wanted him to know they weren't going to take this lying down.

"I heard she resisted arrest and that you assaulted an agent." He *tsked* over the phone. "Are you sure you're not going to be up on charges of your own?"

"I was defending the older woman he grabbed so hard she cried out in pain. These guys are Neanderthals. Horrible government representatives, that's for sure." She'd worked with Homeland for years and the agents tonight were an exception. Someone needed to get a handle on Furniss, and she didn't mind helping get that information up the chain of command. "So, you're saying you're familiar with the case then?"

"It might have crossed my desk." He shuffled some

papers in the background. Lucy could see his office in her mind's eye. He'd framed every award he'd ever been given and papered his walls with them. Modesty definitely wasn't in his vocabulary.

"What can we do to get this taken care of? Daniela Gutierrez needs to be home in her own bed tonight." Lucy waited, knowing James would be thinking through the angles, trying to decide what was in it for him.

"I don't think there's much that can be done. I can't step on another agent's case." But he didn't sound convinced, and so Lucy decided to use the only thing she had to tip the scales in Daniela's favor.

"You know, since I came home, I've had reporters hounding me to do a tell-all about my time in Colombia. They're offering a pretty good paycheck to go on camera and say what I know about the inside workings of a government sting. News on the war on drugs is always good TV."

The words hung for a moment. "Are you threatening to go public with a classified op? You'd be exposed your-self, you know."

"Not at all," she said sweetly. "My uncle's and father's murders by the cartel could be brought out. None of that is classified." She paused for a little dramatic effect. "But then, the government probably wouldn't want the press digging too deep on that score, would they?" She'd long ago accepted that their deaths had been chalked up as casualties of the war on drugs, but sometimes she wanted closure—justice for them. James knew that's why she'd agreed to do undercover work in the first place. She wasn't bluffing about this. If she had to go on the run for the rest of her life, it might be worth it if she made things right for Daniela. "I know we might need some extra cash to get a good lawyer for Daniela, and those reporters will pay a pretty good chunk of it I think." And serve as a little reminder that James wasn't the only one who knew something that could be used as leverage.

"There's no way Bart or his mother needs money, last I heard. Nico set them up before he died with about $25 million." James paused. "But there are some rumblings that Hector Martinez is taking over now and he wants Nico's nephew Manny to be by his side. To make it look good."

Lucy knew about Manny, but couldn't hold back her gasp at the other name. "Hector? He was a lowly drug runner. How could he be behind anything?" Hector was a small, wiry man who always seemed to be watching everything and never spoke. From what she recalled of him, he just ran his route and kept his head down.

"The information I have says that when Nico died, other cartels started moving in on his territory. Hector had just enough connections to block that from happening. With no blood ties, though, he needs Manny to add legitimacy to his bid to rule the cartel and stop an all-out war before there's no Castillo territory to fight for."

She still couldn't believe it. "Hector was always so quiet. I would never have guessed he had any aspirations to leadership."

"Money changes people, you know that. Let me check some details." The clacking of keys came over the phone. "From what I can see, Daniela's been in regular contact with Manny for five weeks. She had to know that wasn't a good idea." He paused for a moment. "Hmm…it looks like Manny dropped off the grid two days ago. If I were a betting man, that's why they're worried. They're probably using her to lure him out and make sure he's not planning any attacks like Nico's last one."

Lucy looked up at Bart. He wasn't going to like this. His fingers were already drumming the desk, waiting for her news. "I got to know Hector pretty well. Maybe I could reach out to him, bypass Manny altogether. Would Homeland be interested in that?"

Bart stood at her words, shaking his head. "No. Absolutely not. You're not going back to that life."

She pressed the phone closer to her ear and turned away from Bart. "James?" If she had to go back to get Daniela out, she would, no matter what Bart said. She knew what it was like to lose a mother and would do everything she could to make sure that didn't happen to Bart.

"You know we'd be interested in that. Since Manny is probably with Hector, we would kill two birds with one stone. Find one, find the other." James's smug tone was back. "Of course I'm not in charge of any of this, but I can make a few phone calls. Recommend you, if you know what I mean."

"I want Daniela Gutierrez released immediately. That's

non-negotiable." Lucy held up a hand to Bart, who was frowning fiercely.

"It'll be nice to work with you again, Lucy. Welcome back." The line went dead, and she froze for just a second. Had that been their plan all along? To lure her back into being an informant? She slowly put her phone away. If so, the plan had worked.

"What was that about?" Bart asked as he stalked over to stand in front of her.

She stood to face him. "I'm going to help them track down Hector Martinez. He's taken over the cartel and is trying to use Manny to solidify his position. Family connections and all."

"They don't need you for that." He placed his hands on her shoulders. "You're out of that life. Doing something that makes you happy. Don't throw that away. We can figure out something else to help my mom."

"I think this might have been their plan all along," Lucy admitted. "They know I don't have any family and that I settled with you and Daniela. They must have thought . . ." Her voice trailed off. It always came down to what you could hold over someone's head. No matter what world you were in, cartel or government, it all came down to leverage.

"So they're using you and my mom." He turned, his fists clenched. "We can't let them do this. It's not right."

She ran her hands down his back. "They justify everything with their mantra that it's for the greater good. In their defense, though, sometimes it is. And with all the things I don't like about James Argyle, he is going to help us," she said softly. "So, no matter what his ulterior motives are, I'd do anything for Daniela. Even if it means working with Homeland again or making a call to Hector. Or both."

He turned back and pulled her to him, cradling the nape of her neck with his palm. "It's so dangerous. He might know you were an informant, and his position is precarious, which will make him reckless and out to prove himself."

Her chest squeezed. That was the one thing she'd hated most about undercover work: trying to gauge danger levels at any given moment. In Nico's world, tempers were always fast and volatile. She didn't think Hector's would be any different. "He probably doesn't know I was an informant. Everyone thinks I was arrested and jailed along with all the top level people. Everything happened so fast, he probably hasn't given me a second thought." Hopefully Manny had kept his mouth shut.

"What reason would you give for reaching out to him?"

His hand was stroking her hair now, making it hard to concentrate. She'd been on her own with no one to count on for so long. Allowing herself to love Bart and let him in had made her vulnerable, but at the same time, he was her strength. With him by her side she could do anything, but for the first time in her life, she was afraid to go forward without him. The fear of losing what they had came back with a vengeance. What if she wasn't meant to be happy?

"I could tell him I got out for good behavior or something and heard he might need me. Hector knew I handled a lot of things for Nico. Maybe he'd want that, too. I could arrange a meeting about it, anyway."

His hand stilled. "I don't like this."

"Neither do I." She leaned back to look him in the eye. "But if it will get your mother back home, I'll do what I have to."

"I still think we should fight, come at them in a way they're not expecting." The muscle in his jaw was working as he looked over her head, trying to work out a solution.

"Who? The cartel or Homeland?" She let her hand move over his back in soothing circles.

Her touch seemed to bring him back to the present. "Both." His put his forehead to hers and let out a long sigh. "I can't believe we're even discussing this. I had an airtight deal with Homeland last time I agreed to their demands. They can't keep threatening her to get us to do what they want."

"What they have on her looks bad, I get that, and she played into their master plan, which, they obviously knew she would. But what's their end game?" She put her hands on either side of his face, feeling the stubble, knowing he felt responsible and it weighed heavily on him. "If you're going to shake up their master plan, I want in. What do you have in mind?"

"I've got an idea that just might work. But Homeland won't like it." His jaw set with determination, his bronze-brown eyes meeting hers. "Hear me out before you decide on anything, okay? I'd rather not have you go this alone, or with only Homeland for backup."

She tilted his face and pressed her lips to his. "You know, you might not have to work too hard to convince me. We make an awesome team."

He smiled and let his hand run down her arms. "Glad we're on the same page, then. Let's get started. We don't have much time."

She took a deep breath as she followed him back to the desk. She could definitely get used to having Daniela and Bart as her family. And she'd do whatever it took to preserve that and keep them safe.

CHAPTER FIVE

Bart sat in the captain's office and watched Lucy methodically make call after call to different cartel members that had escaped prosecution thus far. She slipped right back into that persona seamlessly, but this time it didn't scare him as much as she cajoled and maneuvered the conversation until she got the information she needed. They weren't even wise to her end game. Just seeing a small glimpse of how she operated, it was easy to see how she'd stayed undercover so long. She was a natural, but that was her job, not her. Just as he slipped into his hours of officer training and muscle memory whenever he was in a hostage situation, she did the same. Somehow the parallel between the two had escaped him before, but now offered him some reassurance.

"I got it," she said, hanging up and turning toward him triumphantly. "Hector is in Laredo."

Bart straightened at the unexpected news. "He's in the U.S.? That's pretty risky, especially if Manny is with them. Wouldn't he be afraid Manny would try to escape or the authorities would catch up with him?"

"He wrangled a meeting with Gulf cartel leaders, and they insisted on being in the U.S., so he's using a Castillo safehouse near the border." She stood. "He's only going to be there for twenty-four hours, though, so if we want to catch him, we have to act fast."

That made it doubly risky in Bart's mind. Security would be tight if two cartel leaders were meeting, but they didn't have a lot of other options if they wanted to get Manny back. He locked his eyes on Lucy. "Are you okay with our cover?" She hadn't said much when he'd suggested it. "It makes sense to use my position as Nico's son and yours as his former PR person, now loyal to me."

She nodded. "I know. It's just a volatile situation. You'll definitely be a target if the Gulf cartel leadership is there."

"I'm not worried about myself. If this works, we'll get Manny back and sever the last ties we have to the cartel." Bart was confident in the plan, but Lucy was biting her lip and he could see concern in her eyes. He took her hand, wishing they didn't have to do this at all. He'd rather be delivering flowers to another wedding with her and moving forward in their own relationship.

"Are you sure your team is up for this?" She squeezed his hand. "Not that they aren't qualified, but they probably haven't handled something like this before."

"You'd be surprised. But no matter what, they'll be

there for me, and you won't find a better team anywhere." He stood and touched her arm. "Don't worry. We're going to be fine."

"I'm going to worry, Bart. I don't want to lose you. I've watched your father's people up close for nearly five years. It was ugly. Just the thought of going back and bringing you into it . . ." She shuddered. "This could all go south very quickly and I don't want anything to happen to you."

He took her by the shoulders, letting one hand slide around her shoulder blades and pull her close against his chest. "It's going to be okay. You know them from the inside. We'll get them from the outside. At the first opportunity, we'll grab Manny, and, if we can, turn Hector over to Homeland. I still can't believe he's in the U.S. Our plan will be infinitely easier to execute in this country, rather than having to travel down to Colombia."

She leaned in and put her head on his shoulder. "Are you sure you don't want to wait for Homeland?"

"They have their own agenda, and somehow I don't think their priority is getting Manny out of there." He ran his fingers through her hair and hoped the motion soothed a bit of her anxiety. "I don't want them having any leverage to use on you or to try to draw you back into that life somehow. We can do this on our own terms and avoid all that."

"It seems so logical when you say it like that." Her arms tightened around him. "I was just starting to enjoy being normal."

He tipped her head back and kissed her. Her lips were so soft and yielding, hiding the tough exterior she'd worked so hard to build with her profession. He gathered her in his arms, wanting to be closer. A normal life meant they could be together, that they had a future, and that's what he wanted most. "We're going to finish this. I want you to have a normal life. With me."

She sighed and touched her forehead to his. "I like the sound of that."

The captain cleared his throat from the doorway, quirking an eyebrow at Bart. "Excuse me for interrupting, but Colby and Claire are waiting for us in the interrogation room."

"We'll be right there." Lucy slipped away from him, a flush creeping up her neck.

Bart waited until the captain was gone, then tugged her hand until she was beside him again. "It's okay, you know."

She shook her head. "It's not professional. I don't want your captain questioning your judgment or anything else you do in an official capacity because we're in a relationship." She glanced back at the doorway the captain had just vacated.

"Captain Reed's not like that. He knows what you did as an undercover operative, and he admires you. You never have to worry about him judging you." He smiled at her, willing her to believe him. "Not to mention, this operation is definitely off-book. Let's go brief everyone on our plan, shall we?"

They walked down the hall together, and Bart felt a sense of well-being having her at his side. *We can do this.* A small part of him acknowledged going in and representing himself as Nico's heir ready to take over the Castillo cartel could get dicey, but he pushed that thought away. He had to concentrate on the things he had control over and right now, that meant planning as much of the operation as possible.

They walked into the interrogation room together. Claire, Colby, and the captain were all sitting around the table. Claire had a notebook in front of her. As the main negotiator, she always had a notebook with her, to jot down profile notes, thoughts, and ideas that came to her during hostage situations. The fact she had it with her now made what they were about to do feel more real somehow. They were walking into a situation with just as much potential for a bad outcome as any hostage call they'd been on.

"Did you find out where he is?" Colby asked.

"Laredo," Lucy said, her gaze fixed on Bart. "But only for the next twenty-four hours."

He took it from there. "Homeland is pretty sure Manny will be with him, so the sooner we get down there, the better chance we have of getting him back before they head home to Colombia." Bart pulled up a chair next to Lucy, and they both sat down.

Claire got her pen ready. "So what's the plan?"

"We'll get to the safehouse," Bart said, looking around the table. "If we have time, scope it out just a bit before

Lucy takes me in. She'll tell Hector that I've changed my mind and am ready to take over my father's empire. Hector will have no choice but to at least talk to me. When I've got him distracted, Lucy will get Manny out, and I'll be right behind him."

"Lots of holes in that plan," Claire said, as she jotted down some notes. "What if Hector won't see you? What if Lucy can't find Manny?"

Bart tilted his head to get a better look at Claire while he addressed her concerns. "Hector wants legitimacy, and he needs a Castillo to really have that, but he wants someone he can control. That wouldn't be me. I'm betting he'll trot out Manny to boast that he doesn't need me. When he does, we'll make our move."

"You're betting your life on it." Colby lowered his eyebrows. "What's your exit strategy?"

"Lucy will come up with an excuse to get Manny alone. Ask him to show her the way to the bathroom, whatever. She just needs a little time with him to get out safely. I'll wait a few minutes and be right behind them. When we're back at the airport, we'll give Homeland a heads up." Bart wanted to take Lucy's hand for reassurance, but she was already reaching for Claire's notebook.

"May I?" Lucy asked. Claire nodded and pushed it toward her. Lucy began to sketch. "We know he's at the Castillo stronghold in Laredo, just on the outskirts of town. When I was there last, it looked abandoned, but it has high security. This is a crude sketch, but to scale so you'll get the point."

When she was finished, she pointed to her drawing. "This corner room has extra security. If Hector doesn't have Manny at the meeting, I think that's where Manny will be."

"Both Lucy and I will be able to get past the first level of security on the basis of who we are. It might be a little tougher on the inside, but she'll be my backup if anything goes wrong." And he would be hers. Bart glanced over at her, and she smiled as if she could read his thoughts.

Lucy pointed to the top of the paper. "There's a road here with rotating security. Colby and Claire, you'll be positioned here near an entrance to underground tunnels where you'll breach the safehouse." She made a path with the pen. "Make your way to this area, and you should be able to get close to us. Then, wait for our signal."

"What kind of signal were you thinking?" Colby asked. "You can't be wired. Hector will be looking for that."

"Give us an hour. If we can't get Manny out by then, we'll need your help. That will be the signal." Bart hoped it wouldn't come to that.

"What if the situation escalates before the hour is up and we can't get to you? Is there a Plan B?" Claire asked.

"Yeah, you guys get out of there and don't look back." Bart was adamant about that. He didn't want to be responsible for them getting hurt or trying to be heroes saving him.

"We're not leaving you there." Colby shook his head, vehemently. "Not going to happen."

"I can find my way home, you know that." He caught Colby's eye. "I don't want you hurt."

"You're not my babysitter," Colby growled. "I can take care of myself."

Lucy held up her hand. "Boys. There's too many 'what ifs' to worry about as it is. Let's not borrow trouble. The underground tunnel is our secret weapon. We can stall any escalation until you're in place. I know we can. And if anything goes wrong, you'll be the cavalry coming to our rescue."

"Now that's something I can work with," Claire said, taking back her notebook to look at Lucy's sketch again. "What are we waiting for?"

"I wish I could go," the captain said, regret etched in the lines of his face. "But I'll cover for the three of you while you're gone. Homeland has already reached out, wanting to meet with me later this morning to talk about your mother's release. You better get going if you don't want them to realize what's really going on or make your mother worry more than she already is. If I get a chance, I'll visit her myself."

"Thanks, Cap'n." Bart leaned forward, looking at each person around the table until his gaze stopped at Lucy. She fit there with the team. His team. And he trusted her with his life as much as he did the other three people seated around her. "Let's do this."

CHAPTER SIX

The plane ride to Laredo was filled with an air of apprehension, but with Bart by her side, Lucy felt a layer of comfort she'd never had before. She squeezed his hand. "You still awake?"

He turned and gave her a half-smile. "As if I could sleep. I'm surprised you haven't tried to rest more, though."

"I just want this over with so we can get back to where we were." Her heart did a slow roll as she lifted her free hand to his cheek.

He leaned in and kissed the inside of her wrist, letting his lips linger long enough to make her want to redirect him to her mouth.

"Yeah, I was liking where we were, too," he said as he drew back. "If I have my way, this will be a quick in and out, and we'll be right back on this plane headed home."

She turned toward him, but before she could say

anything, Colby approached and sat in the seat across from them. "We'll be landing in a few minutes. Were you able to get those last few details taken care of?"

Lucy shifted her attention away from Bart. "I have two cars waiting for us on the ground. Bart and I will go in the first one and you guys will take the second. Follow the map I outlined for you and make sure you're not followed."

Bart leaned forward. "We all need to be extra careful. Cartels aren't known for their welcoming committees," he said grimly. "We don't want this thing over before it starts."

"We just have to keep our heads long enough to grab Manny and get out of there," she reminded him. "Play smart."

"We'll give you an hour, and then we're coming in," Colby said, tilting his head down in a no-nonsense position. "I'm not waiting an extra minute, no matter what."

"Hopefully we'll be meeting you at the tunnels long before the time is up." Bart straightened in his seat. "I've been trying to think of a stronger contingency plan that didn't include just waiting for a time signal, but my gut is saying to go with it." He ran a hand over his face. "If Hector has something else planned, I can't think of what it would be."

Lucy rubbed her palms down the front of her slacks. "Hector is all about money and position. He's risen from being a runner to running the empire, so we have to work that angle. Tell him what he wants to hear while we get the information we need." She glanced back at Bart. "It'll be like a walk in the park."

"A walk I don't want you to take," Bart said softly. "But I'm grateful. No matter what, Manny is family, and we'll get him back together."

Lucy didn't miss Colby's indulgent smile as he listened to their conversation. She knew Bart's partner was happy they'd found each other, and she was glad he'd accepted her so readily.

"I'll let you two talk this over while I get ready for landing," Colby said as he stood and returned to his seat.

Bart buckled his seat belt, and Lucy took his hand again. "I'd do anything for you and your family, you know that, right?"

His eyes were shadowed, and she couldn't read his feelings. Did he understand why she was doing this? That his family was hers?

He brushed his thumb over the back of her hand. "When I go into a hostage negotiation, I can usually stay objective to get the job done. I'm good at what I do, but I'm worried that with you and Manny there, something might go wrong. What if I get distracted and put the whole mission in danger?"

"You can't think like that. In five years of undercover work, the one thing I learned was if you stay confident, you can talk your way out of almost anything. We need to keep Hector talking." She bit her lip to stall herself from voicing any of her own concerns. Was his feeling a foreboding? Or just nerves? Her own doubts about doing this on their own started to surface, but she pushed them back. She lifted her chin and took her own advice. *Stay confident.*

"Promise me that if anything goes wrong, you'll get to the tunnels. Don't wait for me." His thumb had stopped the caressing circles and now gripped her hand. He looked so earnest. How could she turn him down?

"I won't leave you to face anything alone. We're a team." She gripped his hand just as tightly. "Whatever happens today, it'll be to both of us standing there."

As the plane touched down, he didn't have time to argue. Her stomach did a little stutter stop like the plane now rumbling toward the gate. She meant what she said about doing this together. The only question now was whether they'd both make it through.

She took one last look out the plane window, the sun starting to rise and push the night away. Being undercover in the cartel had been a stifling darkness, and she hadn't realized how dark it really had been until she'd gotten out. This was her chance to fight for the dream of a home, family, and love. A life of light that included Bart standing by her side.

And this was where she'd make her stand to keep that dream alive.

CHAPTER SEVEN

Bart cracked his knuckles as they drove up the long driveway to the compound Hector was hiding in. The estate must have been opulent in its day, but by the weak lights set strategically around the grounds, the sprawling two-story house looked run down and uninhabited. The Spanish tile roof was missing quite a few tiles, and the stuccoed arches were peeling. Overgrown grass and weeds were everywhere. If he hadn't seen security, he would have thought it was abandoned.

The security they'd run across had been what he'd expected. Guards were posted strategically around the house. One pair had stopped them and checked the car before waving them through. When they heard Bart's name, though, there was an air of expectation. As Nico Castillo's son, he couldn't get used to the range of emotions his name evoked in people. For some in law enforcement, it was anger and disgust at the criminal activities Nico had engaged in. In the drug cartel world, it was respect and a sort of honor. It was up to Bart to adjust his thinking for this situation.

Claire and Colby had taken the second car at the airport as planned, and hopefully they were getting to the secret tunnels about now. If anything went wrong they'd have his back, but the goal was to get all of them on that plane with Manny sitting next to them, laughing about how easy that had been. He put every other doubt in a lockbox in his head and focused on that image. *Positive thinking.*

He glanced over at Lucy. She had on a light blue blouse that looked silky with black dress pants. He'd seen her wear similar clothing when they'd been on the island off Colombia. It was like her signature outfit when she'd worked for the cartel. She was back in that world, her game face on. *But,* he reminded himself, *it's a job.* Just like the Hostage Negotiation Team was his, but his uniform didn't define every aspect of his life, and neither did hers. It did make him hold the private moments they'd shared closer to his heart, though, like her smile when she was working at the shop, her laugh at his mother's matchmaking, or the soft look in her eyes when he kissed her. That's what he was fighting for—the privilege of having that hope and promise between them as part of his life and family.

They got out, and before they'd even gone up the crumbling stone steps, the front door opened. "Ms. Aguayo," the guard murmured to her as they entered. He patted them down and ran a wand over them. Bart tamped down his annoyance watching the guy run his hands up Lucy's legs, but she looked unperturbed.

"*Hola*, Alberto." She stopped. "Where is he?"

Alberto didn't even ask who she was referring to. "Waiting for you in the library. You remember. Third door on your right."

Bart took her elbow, grateful for the contact that seemed innocuous enough, but settled his nerves. "You know him?" He whispered and jerked his thumb back at Alberto.

"He used to be another runner. Maybe being a guard for Hector is a step up," she whispered back.

They walked through the hall, the once-proud murals of bull-fighters now faded and shabby, large sections fallen to the floor. "Has it always been like this?" he asked, gesturing to the walls.

"It's gotten worse." She stopped at the third door. "There's no reason to fix it up. It's a way station and people tend to bother you less if they think no one lives here or that it's even livable."

She gave a cursory knock and walked in. Bart stayed close, just in case Hector was planning an ambush. He wished there had been some way to smuggle in a gun, but having his backup team waiting would have to be enough. Hector stood near the empty fireplace, Manny seated in front of him and two guards stood in the corners. The only light was from the dingy windows throughout the room. No sign of any Gulf cartel members. Maybe they'd missed that meeting or it hadn't happened yet.

Manny gave them a crooked smile, his eyes wide and unnaturally bright. Was he high at this time of morning? *At least we don't have to wonder where he is*, Bart thought.

"Hector," he said mildly, crossing the room to face him. "Thanks for agreeing to a meeting on such short notice."

Hector grunted. "Lucy said you are planning to take your father's place. I'm here to tell you that won't be possible." He was a small man, but compact, his body solid muscle. Bart didn't want to underestimate him.

Lucy came to stand next to him. She tucked her hair behind her ear and looked Hector in the eye. "Bart has a legitimate claim, you know that. Frankly, I was surprised to hear you even attempted to take Nico's place."

Hector nodded toward Manny. "I have Nico's nephew who understands the business intimately. We have the legitimate claim." He folded his arms and tapped his fingers on his bicep. "Bart here has no idea what he's getting into or what this position entails. And didn't I hear he's a cop? Not that that means anything, as we all know, but he walked away once. All he has to do is walk away again."

Bart stepped forward. "I know more than you think, and I'm not walking away. I'm the rightful heir, and the other cartel heads know it. They won't give you the time of day once I tell them you're trying to set yourself up in my place."

Manny attempted to stand up, but Hector put his hand on his shoulder, forcing him to stay in his seat.

Bart couldn't wait to get Manny away from this whole situation, but it was hard to be patient. "I'd like to speak to my cousin alone."

Manny tried to squirm away, but Hector squeezed his shoulder. "Now that I see you're serious, I'd be happy to let you talk to your cousin. Or take him home."

Bart resisted the urge to look at Lucy. Surely it couldn't be this easy.

Hector barely took a breath. "For the price of $25 million dollars. I deserve that much. If it wasn't for me, you wouldn't have anything left to take over. Everyone is encroaching on Castillo territory. I kept them away."

Hector's demand didn't surprise Bart at all, but his reasons did. "Why do you care about my father's business?"

"It's all I've ever known, and I had a chance to partner with Manny and run it how it should have been run—as an empire!" He shook a fist.

Hector's eyes widened as he ranted and he ran a hand through his hair until it stuck up around his ears. Bart was getting concerned. Maybe Hector had a drug issue as well. It was hard to tell.

Manny shook off Hector's hand and stood, reaching for the arm of the chair to steady himself. "I can still do it," he said petulantly. He stared angrily at Bart. "You always think you're better than me. Well, this time I'm going to prove I can do something better than you." He staggered toward Lucy and grasped her shoulders. "You believe in me, don't you, Lucy? You always did."

Bart's watched her try to hide a grimace at Manny's tight hold and felt his chest squeeze like iron bands were cutting off his air. "Let her go, Manny. Now." His voice came out a little louder than he wanted, but he resisted the urge to shove Manny away from her.

Too late he realized that he'd turned his attention away from Hector. Before he could focus, he heard the soft click of a gun near his ear. Bart put his hands up in a conciliatory manner.

"You can all go, as soon as I get my money," Hector hissed. "If I can't have the cartel, I'll take what I'm owed for a nice retirement."

Bart's back was to the door, but his eyes were on Lucy and Manny. "Let's talk about this, Hector. Maybe we can split the money."

Lucy's eyes darted to the door behind him and widened. In that split second, he knew something was wrong. Instinct took over and he ran toward her, right before the flash grenade went off.

CHAPTER EIGHT

Lucy ducked down at the same time Bart rushed to cover her with his body, only a heartbeat before the explosion. Her ears were ringing, and she lay still for a moment to get her bearings. That's all the time they had, though, before the shooting started.

"Get Manny," she said loudly, twisting in Bart's arms.

Gunshots filled the room, and Lucy didn't see Manny right away. When she spotted him, he was still by the fireplace, half-hidden behind the armchair. Bart must have seen him, too, because they moved toward him simultaneously, keeping their heads down.

Hector and his guards were behind two sofas near the far corner of the room and they were completely focused on returning fire. Manny was less than ten feet away, but it seemed like an eternity before they got there. Bart reached out and grabbed his arm. "Let's get out of here."

"We need to get to that last wall panel," Lucy said,

leaning close to Bart. "There's a spring lock that will lead to the tunnels."

"I can't go," Manny said, looking wildly at them. "Hector says I have to prove myself or something." He pushed back, but Bart held him fast.

"You're coming. We've risked everything to get you out of here, and I'm not leaving you behind." He pulled Manny's arm. "Three musketeers, remember? We don't have to prove anything to anyone. We're a team."

Manny seemed to calm at those words as if they pierced the drug-filled haze he was in. "Three musketeers. All for one." He reached for Lucy's hand, his face clearing as if he was coming back to himself. "Okay. Let's go."

Lucy let out a breath of frustrated relief as they inched toward the hidden door. Hector's two guards were still in their defensive positions around the room, and she could see a clean-cut man near the bottom of the doorway, with another one at the top returning fire. Who were these guys? But when she saw their navy blue HSI jacket, she answered her own question. How had Homeland Security found them?

At first she'd thought it was Claire and Colby who had gone on the offensive early, but it hadn't been an hour yet. Not that she knew exactly how much time had elapsed; she hadn't really been keeping track. She only knew that time had stood still when Hector held that gun to Bart's head. That was a moment she never wanted to relive.

The last two feet before the wall panel put them in Hector's line of sight. Did they dare risk it? She looked back for verification from Bart, but they didn't have a lot of other choices.

"Throw down your weapons," a voice commanded from the doorway. "Now."

Hector's answer was to fire on the officers again. Maybe the flash bang had affected his hearing, but more than likely, he had always planned to shoot his way out. Using the distraction, Lucy made a beeline for the wall panel. She slid her finger along the top, searching for the spring lock, when the panel opened on its own. Colby was on the other side with Claire right behind him, her gun at the ready.

"Are you both okay?" Colby asked in an urgent whisper. She nodded. "Let's get you guys out of there, then."

Lucy reached back for Manny, but Bart signaled for her to go first. She did as he asked, Manny right behind her. As soon as he was through, she reached for Bart, but the room behind them, which had been deafening since the gun fight broke out, suddenly went silent. Bart glanced back, then started to close the panel, as if he were going to sacrifice his safety for hers. Lucy pushed the panel back. "No way. We do this together."

He stared at her and deep inside she knew this was a moment she'd remember forever. She held her breath. The darkness around her faded away as she was drawn to the light surrounding Bart. "Just remember, I love you," he said, his voice low, but clear.

Her heart tripped over itself. She'd waited so long to hear those words. From the crush she'd had on him as a girl, through all the lonely years as a young adult. And when he finally said them, they were in a cartel way station in the middle of a gunfight. It all felt a little unreal and her tongue was frozen to the roof of her mouth. She couldn't say anything.

She was quickly snapped back to reality when a commanding voice behind Colby said, "Stand up." Lucy couldn't place it. Was it a guard? Homeland?

"Watch him," she said to Colby, pointing at Manny before she scrambled out of the tunnel to join her fate to Bart's. She would keep her promise that whatever happened today would be to both of them.

She stood up quickly to see that the man pointing a gun at them was a Homeland agent, not one of Hector's men. He wasn't familiar, but the Special Agent in Charge walking behind him was. Every defensive instinct she had rose up in her. "James, what's going on?"

He shook his head. "You know, there were bets as to whether you'd lead us to Hector. I told them you wouldn't go without us. Cost me ten bucks." He came over to stand in front of Lucy. "I thought you trusted me."

"You practically kidnapped Daniela to get your way. How would that make me trust you?" She folded her arms, not letting his cockiness get to her. She'd dealt with him for too long as her handler to let that bother her anymore. "We did what we thought was best. How did you find us?"

"We had you under surveillance."

"No way." Bart was adamant. "I made sure we didn't have a tail."

"Homeland has a few more resources available to us than the local police force. You wouldn't have seen what we had on you." James shifted as more agents came into the room. "Since we're playing twenty questions, how did you know exactly where to find Hector?"

"I called in a few favors," Lucy told him.

"People you've already reported to Homeland on your debriefing, I hope." He cocked an eyebrow at her. "No secret contacts, right?"

"Of course not." Lucy looked around, wondering why he was shifting so much. Then she saw the scene directly behind him.

Hector was on the floor, obviously dead. Part of her was relieved, but the other part just felt sad at more death. If she never had to see another dead body in her lifetime, that would be fine with her. "What are your plans now that Hector's taken care of? You know someone else will step in to take his place."

"This business is like trying to hold back a sandstorm with a flyswatter. It feels futile at times, but for every piece of sand we take care of, there's a little less flying in our face, you know? We'll just keep going after them one by one." James took a step toward the door. "I'm going to need to take your cousin in for questioning," he said to Bart.

At that, Bart straightened and closed the distance between him and James. "No. I'm drawing the line. You used us. You used my mother. I'm done. I want you to leave my family alone. I'll take care of my cousin, and I never want to hear from you or Homeland again."

Lucy had never heard him sound so fierce, but she agreed with every word. "He's right. It's over, James."

He had the grace to hang his head slightly. "I'm sorry about your mom, okay? That did cross a line, and I let the higher-ups know. I don't think Miller will be a Special Agent in Charge much longer, and Furniss will be lucky to get away with a write-up in his file. You have to understand, though, we needed to get to Hector before he had his meeting with the other cartel heads, and we accomplished that. If we wait long enough, we might even get a crack at arresting the head of the Gulf cartel." He looked back at the dead man and then faced Bart. "I want you to know I dropped your mother off at her home personally, and I give you my word we won't bother you anymore."

Bart folded his arms, his glare enough to make any man flinch. After an extra moment, he held out a hand and James shook it. "I've heard that promise before. I want it in writing and signed by you and your boss," Bart said adamantly. "I'm not taking any more chances with you people and your words."

"Fine, fine." James waved a hand in the air as if that was a given. The small door panel opened again and Claire and Manny came out. Manny was shaking and went immediately to Bart's side. "Is this real?" His hands shook as he took in the scene around them.

Bart put his arm around him, his voice soothing. "Don't worry. I'm going to take care of you, Manny."

"Colby's waiting in the driveway," Claire said. "The sooner we get out of here, the better. Homeland can take care of the rest."

Lucy walked behind Bart and Manny, stepping over an upturned side table, but Bart stopped and reached back for her. "Thanks," he said, his eyes soft. "I couldn't have done this without you."

Her heart warmed at his words. "Let's go home."

CHAPTER NINE

After searching for a rehab center that would meet Manny's needs and getting him settled there, they were grateful to finally be home. Bart sat across from Lucy, watching her clip the stems off flowers as she put together a bouquet. They'd both insisted Daniela take a few days off to recover from her ordeal while Lucy took care of things at the shop. She was doing a good job, too. Bart couldn't stop staring at her. Ever since they'd come back from Laredo, it was as if a light had been turned on inside of her. She couldn't stop smiling, and that made him a happy man.

"What?" she asked, raising her eyebrows.

"Nothing." He picked up a discarded flower and twirled it in his hand. "What are these? They smell so good."

"You mean you don't recognize them from your mom's logo? The store's named after them."

"Forget-me-nots? For some reason I thought they'd be bigger."

"They're small, but they have a stronger fragrance at night. I love it." She clipped another one. "But that's not what you were thinking about."

"Can't I just admire a beautiful woman?"

She laughed, crinkling her nose up. "My hair is in a messy bun, and I'm wearing an apron."

He leaned over the table and held out the forget-me-not. "It doesn't matter what you're wearing. You are beautiful. Inside and out."

She took the bud and lifted it to her nose. "Sweet talker." But she met him halfway and slipped her hand around his neck, pulling him closer. "I still love you, though."

He cupped her jaw tenderly and kissed her. She smelled like roses and forget-me-nots, and he couldn't get enough of her, even with a work table between them. "I love you, too," he said when they broke apart. He sat back in his chair, his eyes turning serious. "I did want to discuss something with you."

A crease appeared in her brow and she settled on her work stool. "Sounds serious."

"It is." His pulse picked up. He wanted her to love his idea, but now the time had come to tell her, and he was feeling nervous. "I've been doing some checking. The money my father left me was from his philanthropic endeavors, so it's clean." He tilted his chin down and took a breath. "I've been thinking. What if I started a foundation with the money? To give grants for drug addiction and recovery centers that focus on whole families as well as the addict. I can't get my aunt and Manny out of my head. That whole family needs help." He sucked in a breath, waiting for her reaction.

"You're going to use all the money your father left you to start a foundation that helps those affected by drugs?" Her voice was careful; he couldn't quite read her face.

"Yeah. That's what I was thinking."

She rose and came around the table to stand in front of him. Picking up his hand, she stared down at him still in his chair. "I don't think I could love you any more than I do right now." Her voice was low, nearly a whisper, but his heart nearly pounded out of his chest when his brain registered what she was saying.

"So you approve?" He pulled her closer, wrapping his arms around her waist.

She ran her fingers through his hair. "What better way to exorcise the demons surrounding our past and everything your father stood for than to use his money like that?"

"That actually hadn't occurred to me, but it makes a lot of sense." He stood and wrapped her in his arms, looking at the bouquet she'd been working on with the forget-me-nots. "But there are a few things I'd like to talk about from the past. Things I don't want to forget or let go."

She stiffened. "Oh yeah?"

"You know when we were kids and you claimed you could beat me at any game that included a ball?" He felt her body relax and he stifled a laugh. "Well, I want a rematch. On every single sport."

She laughed out loud and leaned back to look at him. "Anytime. Anyplace." Her whole face was lit up with happiness, and Bart knew his expression mirrored hers. How could he not? He loved her. She'd challenged him and intrigued him from the moment they'd met, and that was just the way he liked it.

"Not right now, though." He bent and nuzzled her neck. "Later. Much, much later, after I've worked out all my distraction techniques."

"You couldn't distract me," she said, but her breathless-ness belied her words. She leaned her head back as he trailed kisses along her jawline. "Maybe *I'm* distracting you."

He lifted his head and grinned at her sassy smile. With a nod, he said, "I may have to rethink this rematch then."

"Or, we could start fresh. You know, since we're both older and wiser." Her eyes twinkled. "Of course, we both know I'll give you a run for your money. I did back then, and I definitely will now."

"I wouldn't have it any other way." He plucked one of the forget-me-nots from the table. "I think these are my new favorite flower," he murmured. "Symbolic of us, really."

And he tucked the blossom behind her ear and kissed her again.

Read More in the Hostage Negotiation Series!

All Fall Down—Navy SEAL Rafe Kelly's brother is kidnapped by dangerous terrorists and he teams with a beautiful hostage negotiator to get his brother back.

Ashes Ashes—Colby Black helps out his mysterious next-door neighbor, Sophia Naziri, and she pulls Colby into a web of lies and conspiracy.

Pocket Full of Posies—Bart Gutierrez accepts a dangerous assignment inside a cartel and discovers a woman from his past—and that a large-scale attack on America is imminent.

Ring Around the Rosie—-Captain Ron Reed is forced to bargain for the lives of his team and his ex-wife, Sarah, the woman he still loves, but will his sacrifice be too little too late?

Julie Coulter Bellon is an award-winning author of over two dozen published books. Her book All Fall Down won the RONE award for Best Suspense, The Captain was a RONE award finalist, and Pocket Full of Posies won a RONE Honorable Mention. Most recently her books, The Capture and Second Look were both Whitney finalists for Best Suspense/Mystery.

Julie loves to travel and her favorite cities she's visited so far are probably Athens, Paris, Ottawa, and London. In her free time, she loves to read, write, teach, watch Hawaii Five-O reruns, and eat Canadian chocolate. Not necessarily in that order.

If you'd like to be the first to hear about Julie's new projects and receive a free book, you can sign up to be part of her VIP group on her website www. juliebellon.com

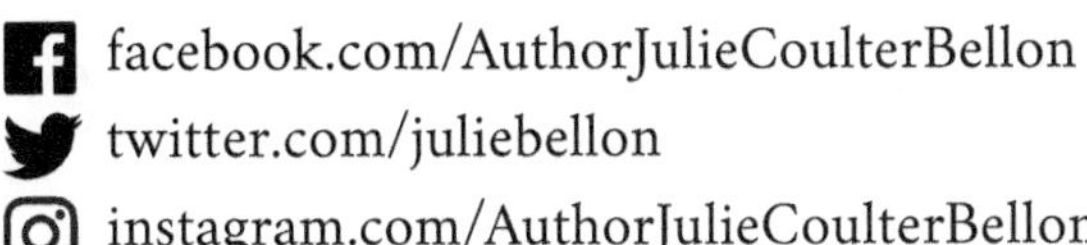

www.ingramcontent.com/pod-product-compliance
Lightning Source LLC
Chambersburg PA
CBHW060600100726
47907CB00005B/1452